Biscuit's Birthday

story by ALYSSA SATIN CAPUCILLI
pictures by PAT SCHORIES

HarperFestival®
A Division of HarperCollins*Publishers*

"Wake up, sleepy Biscuit!" said the little girl.
"Do you know what day it is?"
Woof!

"Today is a very special day.
It's your birthday!"

Woof! Woof!

"Follow me, Biscuit," said the little girl.
"I have something special planned just for you."

"Surprise, Biscuit! Puddles and Daisy are here for your birthday party!"

Bow wow!
Meow!

"Come along, everybody. It's time to play some birthday games."

Woof, woof!
Bow wow!
Meow!

"Silly Biscuit!" called the little girl.
"Be careful with those balloons."

"Oh, no," said the little girl. "There go the balloons!"
Woof!

"Oh, Biscuit!" The little girl laughed. "You may be a year older, but you will always be my silly little puppy."

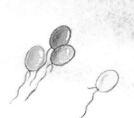

"Now it's time for birthday treats,"
said the little girl.
"Make a wish, Biscuit."

Woof!

"Funny puppy! You want to open your birthday presents!"

"Look, Biscuit! A new collar, a new bone, and best of all . . ."

Woof, woof!

"A new box of biscuits!
Happy birthday, Biscuit!"

Woof!

Word Search

Do you see these words? Circle each one you find.
Be sure to look across and down.

HAPPY BIRTHDAY PARTY CAKE PRESENT TOY

To see the answers, turn to the last page.

H A P P Y C Y P
T F E M R A L A
O J V U Z K Q R
Y P R E S E N T
B I R T H D A Y

Birthday Maze

Help Biscuit find his birthday treat!

Start here.

Happy birthday, Biscuit!

Where's Biscuit?

Connect the dots from one to thirty-four to see what Biscuit is up to.

Color by Numbers with Biscuit!

Following the color key below, use crayons to color in the picture of Biscuit and the little girl.

1=red   3=yellow   5=purple
2=blue   4=green   6=peach

Mixed-up Words

These words are all mixed-up! Can you fix them?
Hint—they're all in the story.

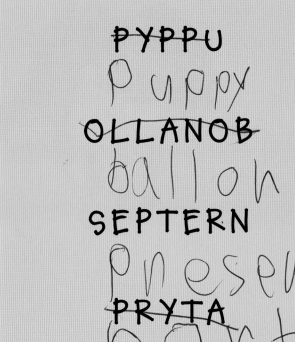

PYPPU
Puppy

OLLANOB
balloh

SEPTERN
present

PRYTA
party

To see the answers, turn to the last page.

Birthday Treats

What will Biscuit and his friends eat at his party?
Circle the pictures of their favorite foods.

Answers

Word Search

H	A	P	P	Y	C	Y	P
T	F	E	M	R	A	L	A
O	J	V	U	Z	K	Q	R
Y	P	R	E	S	E	N	T
B	I	R	T	H	D	A	Y

Birthday Maze

Mixed-up Words

PUPPY

BALLOON

PRESENT

PARTY